Doogie
Gets Lost
Written by
Brenda Arthur
Illustrations by
Don Edstrom
Colour by
Brenda MacDonald

ISBN: Softcover 978-1-4990-1958-2
EBook 978-1-4990-1959-9

Rev. date: 06/24/2014

To order additional copies of this book, contact:
Xlibris LLC
1-888-795-4274
www.Xlibris.com
Orders@Xlibris.com

To my daughters, Brenda, Amanda, Crystal and Dayna.

There was once a baby Dragon named Doogie.

Doogie lived with his parents far away in Dragonville.

One day while playing in the backyard, Doogie found a butterfly. The butterfly was purple, blue, green and pink.

"I wonder where that butterfly lives."
Doogie wondered out loud.

No one answered Doogie, for he was all alone.

Doogie decided to follow the butterfly home. He crawled under the bushes and out the back to the woods behind his house.

Quickly he followed the butterfly into the woods.

Faster and faster the butterfly flew.

Soon, Doogie grew tired and wanted to go home.

He stopped and looked around. He didn't know where he was.

He was lost.

Doogie was very scared and started to cry.

Doogie ran and ran, hoping to find his way home.

After a while he stopped running and started to think.

"Maybe I could see my way home if I climbed a tall, tall tree."
He said to himself.

Doogie looked for the biggest tree he could find.

He looked way up.

Doogie got brave and started to climb.

Higher and higher, up to the top.

Slowly he reached the top. Doogie looked carefully down, then around.

Far away he could see his house. Excited, he quickly climbed down.

Faster and faster, he ran back home.

Under the bushes, and into the backyard.

There was Doogie's Mom. He raced to her and threw his arms around her ankle.

Doogie decided the best place to be was at home.

CPSIA information can be obtained
at www.ICGtesting.com
Printed in the USA
LVIC06n0024090714
393435LV00003B/5
9781499019582